TINY
BARBARIAN

TINY BARBARIAN

WRITTEN BY **AME DYCKMAN**

ILLUSTRATED BY **ASHLEY SPIRES**

HARPER
An Imprint of HarperCollinsPublishers

Library of Congress Cataloging-in-Publication Data

Names: Dyckman, Ame, author. | Spires, Ashley, 1978- illustrator.

Title: Tiny Barbarian / written by Ame Dyckman ; illustrated by Ashley Spires.

Description: First edition. | New York, NY : HarperCollins Children's Books, 2021. |
    Summary: Tiny fantasizes he is a mighty Barbarian who can conquer anything, but
    even he has trouble conquering the dark.

Identifiers: LCCN 2020023316 | ISBN 9780062881649 (hardcover)

Subjects: CYAC: Imagination—Fiction. | Fear of the dark—Fiction.

Classification: LCC PZ7.D9715 Ti 2021 | DDC [E]—cc23

LC record available at https://lccn.loc.gov/2020023316

The artist wielded Photoshop to concuer the art in this book.

21 22 23 24 25   RTLO   10 9 8 7 6 5 4 3 2 1

❖

First Edition

Meet Tiny Barbarian!

Tiny may be tiny, but he's—

MIGHTY!

Tiny has already conquered many things:

Tiny conquered his first word.

He conquered his first steps.

He even conquered the potty.

Tiny has *always* been a conqueror,
but Tiny wasn't *always* Tiny Barbarian.
He's only been a Barbarian since . . .

EARLIER TODAY!

It all started during a nice family walk
and a chat about *the future*.
Tiny's mommy and daddy said
Tiny could be *anything* he wanted.

But Tiny didn't wait for the future.

A BARBARIAN?!

Tiny saw himself defending his realm.
He saw himself protecting his family.
He saw himself with all that *stuff*!

The shining helmet.

The sturdy club.

The flaming torch.

The fuzzy cape in case it got chilly.
(Even mighty Barbarians get chilly.)

YEAH! A BARBARIAN!

He just needed a few things:

The shining helmet.

The sturdy club.

The fuzzy cape
in case it got chilly.

Tiny put them all together and . . .

HERE WE ARE! A mighty Barbarian has emerged!
Ready to defend his realm. Ready to protect his family. Ready to—

CONQUER EVERYTHING!

With his shining helmet and sturdy club and fuzzy cape in case it got chilly, Tiny Barbarian embarked on his quest to—

CONQUER EVERYTHING!

(Well, everything in his backyard.)

But these fearsome foes were no match for Tiny Barbarian!
Tiny Barbarian rose to the challenge and issued his Battle Cry:

Then Tiny Barbarian defeated them *all*!

BOP! The dragon.

BOP! The troll.

BOP! Even the giant broccoli.

His quest complete, our triumphant hero returned home.
His realm? Defended.
His family? Protected.
And he was—

HUNGRY!

(Even mighty Barbarians need to eat their dinner.)

There was a Victory Feast.

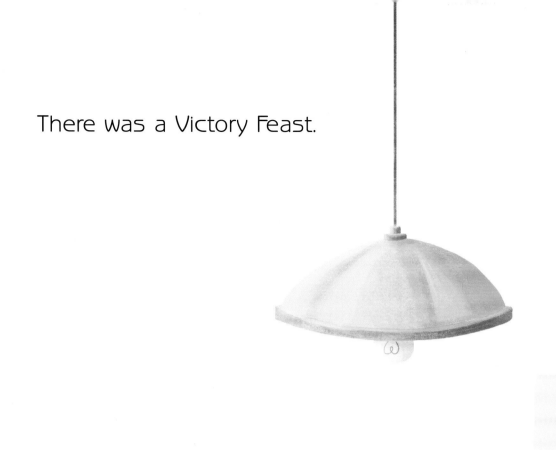

TAKE THAT, BROGGOLI!

There was a Victory Parade.

WOO-HOO! AGAIN!

And then it was time for bed.

NOT SLEEPY!

Now now, Tiny. Even mighty Barbarians need their rest.

CLICK!

Suddenly, Tiny found himself facing his most challenging foe of all:

THE DARK!

And Tiny didn't know how to conquer *THIS*.

HOW DO I BOP
THE DARK?

But Tiny could be brave
and *try*.

Then THE DARK
made a noise.

CREEEAK!

Tiny had no time to grab his shining helmet!
No time to grab his sturdy club!

Instead, he grabbed
his flaming torch!

And Tiny Barbarian
came face-to-face with . . .

CLICK!

KITTY! IT'S YOU!

MEOW!

There was nothing for Tiny Barbarian to fear.
His realm was defended.
His family? Protected.

And he had his Kitty in case he got chilly.

Tiny Barbarian could just be Tiny again.
He could conquer more tomorrow.

Sweet dreams, Tiny.